T0197709

RICO
A ROBOT HERO

Story and illustrations by:

Tony Costanzo

To order additional copies of this book, contact:
Xlibris
844-714-8691
www.Xlibris.com
Orders@Xlibris.com

ISBN: Softcover   978-1-6698-7571-0
        Hardcover   978-1-6698-7572-7
        EBook   978-1-6698-7570-3

Print information available on the last page

Rev. date: 05/18/2023

RICO

A ROBOT HERO

This robot wasn't just parts and metal.

Read about how he proved that to others.

Story and illustrations by:

Tony Costanzo

Author's Message

Robots are used in big business today. Soon they will also help us in our homes. They will do painting, mowing lawns, cleaning and even building things.

This story started in the yard of a busy robot factory.
This factory supplied work robots to the nearby towns.
"Robot 831 get back in line," shouted the angry guard.

Rico, the robot, just wanted to live in the outside world.

He dreamed of being free. His built in computer's voice said,
"You are a lot more than just metal and bolts."

Rico tried to hide a family picture that he had found. He would be in big trouble with the robot police, if they saw it. He looked at the picture a lot.

Rico hoped that maybe someday he would be part of a real family.

It was early morning inspection time. Soon the robots would be sent around the town to work. Suddenly, there was a loud BOOM. Robot 831 had carelessly bumped into a metal ladder. He had damaged a factory computer. "Report for repairs!." shouted the angry guard. Poor Rico was shaking with fear!

Rico saw his chance to get away. He quickly hid inside the lawn robot's grass collection case. The busy guards never even noticed. These robots would be delivered to places around town to work. It was the only way that Rico could escape from the robot factory. He was able to get inside the van.

Soon the van made it's first stop. The lawn mower robot had to mow the lawns around the town's fire station. Out jumped a nervous Rico. He raced toward a small shed. Rico had no idea, however, that someone was watching him. It was Alberto, the fire chief's son. His cat, Muffy, was tangled way up on the building's outside ladder.

There was no time to ask questions. Muffy was in danger. Rico heard the cat crying and went into action. Alberto watched as Rico's ladder-like legs moved him upward. His metal arms held the nervous cat securely. Soon Muffy was safely back on the ground. Alberto was so happy, but what could he say to a robot?

"Follow me to the shed so I can give Muffy some water." said Alberto. He noticed the word FRIEND on Rico's message screen. "Muffy was in a very dangerous spot and you saved him." said Alberto. Rico's computer voice said, "I am more than just a machine and I want to be a part of a family." Alberto was the fire chief's son. He helped at the station after school. He told Rico that he could stay in the shed for now.

Time at the playground with Alberto and his friends was just what Rico needed. This was his first day of real freedom from the robot factory. Imagine seeing a robot swinging on the swings! Rico's computer was also downloading all the great music from the radio. This was way better than all the loud machine noises at the robot factory.

Rico wanted to help the town's people.

He started his own dog walking service.

He picked up litter and trash on the sidewalks.

When your friend is a robot on wheels, you don't need an electric bike with a motor.

You can zoom up and down the hills without even pedaling. Rico towed the kids everywhere.

They even made Rico wear a helmet.

Then one day everything changed. The factory's robot police were patrolling the town. They were handing out Rico's picture with reward money for help capturing him. The town's people had gathered around to pick up the flyers. Even Alberto couldn't believe it. Suddenly, one of the robot police shouted, "There he is!" He shined a big beaming light on Rico who was hiding in the brush nearby.

After a few minutes, there was lightning, wind and even some rain. The town's people left in a hurry. Soon the van moved closer to Rico who was trying to go up a steep hill. They tried to shoot a giant net over him. However, some tree branches got in the way. Rico with his wheels spinning was able to escape.

Somehow, Rico was able to make it back to the fire station's shed. He had a few dents and a twisted antenna, but at least he was safe for now. Rain, wind and lightning pounded the shed's roof. Then he heard a BOOM!

It shook the shed's walls. Something very heavy had hit the ground. Rico, however, was very tired and just fell asleep.

That morning a half asleep Rico heard a loud ringing alarm. He looked out the shed's small window, "Oh no," he thought. "A giant tree had fallen blocking the fire station's big doors." The poor fire fighters couldn't leave to answer the alarm. Within seconds, Rico was outside to help. In the pouring rain Rico's power arms and built -in leg ladders moved the huge tree to the side. With their sirens blaring, the fire fighters sped away.

Rico decide to follow the firefighters. Amazingly, the fire was at the robot factory of all places. He couldn't believe it. Dark smoke, burning oil and huge flames were everywhere. Rico knew the building so well. His computer even showed the fire fighters a map of the inside. This was a great help in rescuing people. Everyone was able to get out safely. After a long weary battle, the fire was finally under control.

A week later, there was a special ceremony to honor the brave firefighters. Both the fire chief and robot police commander gave out awards. Rico's many acts of courage were finally recognized. He moved that giant tree away from the station's doorway. He saved lives at the robot factory fire. Alberto watched proudly while Rico received his medal of bravery. The fire chief went on to say that, Rico would have a place to live at the fire station and be a member of the fire department.

They gave Rico this special picture. It reminded him of the one that he had to always hide at the robot factory.

Look closely and you might notice a tiny tear drop in one of Rico's eyes.

BEING PART OF THE FAMILY IS THE MOST IMPORTANT THING OF ALL.

Printed in the United States
by Baker & Taylor Publisher Services